Penny Dreadful

causes a Kerfuffle

By Joanna Nadin

Illustrated by Jess Mikhail

Contents

Penny Dreadful
and the New Girl

Penny Dreadful's
Top 5 Tips for Survival

Meet Penny Dreadful and her Resigned Relations

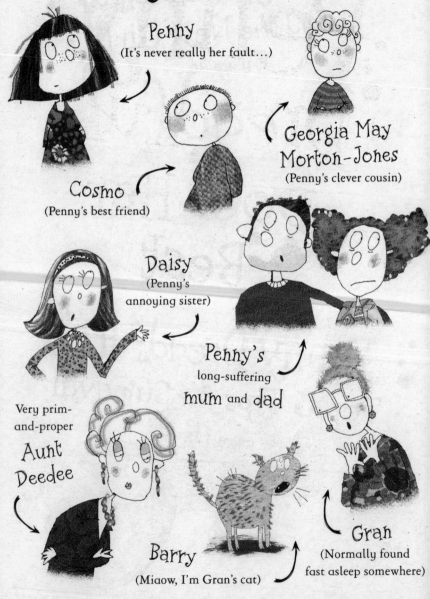

Penny
(It's never really her fault…)

Georgia May Morton-Jones
(Penny's clever cousin)

Cosmo
(Penny's best friend)

Daisy
(Penny's annoying sister)

Penny's long-suffering mum and dad

Very prim-and-proper Aunt Deedee

Barry
(Miaow, I'm Gran's cat)

Gran
(Normally found fast asleep somewhere)

Penny Dreadful

Does Her Best

My name
is not actually
Penny Dreadful. It is Penelope Jones.
The "Dreadful" bit is my dad's **JOKE**. I know it
is a joke because every time he says it he laughs
like a honking goose. But I do not see the funny
side. Plus it is not even true that I am dreadful.

It is like Gran says, i.e. that I am a **MAGNET FOR DISASTER**. Mum says if Gran kept a better eye on me in the first place instead of on *Cough Drop* in the two o'clock at Newmarket then I might not be quite so magnetic. But Gran says if Mum wasn't so busy answering phones for Dr. Cement, who is her boss and who has bulgy eyes like hard-boiled eggs (which is why everyone calls him Dr. Bugeye), and Dad wasn't so busy solving crises at the council, then they would be able to solve some crises at 73 Rollins Road, i.e. our house. So you see it is completely not my fault.

For instance it is completely not my fault that right now I am utterly blueish all over, and so is my best friend Cosmo Moon Webster, and so is my sister Daisy's swan outfit, and so is our best tablecloth. It is probably definitely the fault of Mr. Schumann, our headmaster, who is most often saying things like "Penelope Jones, for the last time spoons are for **EATING WITH** not **BALANCING ON YOUR NOSE**". And it is especially annoying because I was **ONLY TRYING TO HELP**. So here is what happened.

On Friday, Bridget Grimes, who is top of

the class and Mr. Schumann's favourite, is not wearing school uniform (which is red top, grey bottoms, white socks and black shoes that must be **SENSIBLE**) and Miss Patterson, who is our teacher and very tall and thin like a beanpole, does not **EVEN** tell her off. And I do not think this is fair, because Cosmo Moon Webster **DOES** get told off because he is wearing a Jedi outfit, because his mum (who is called

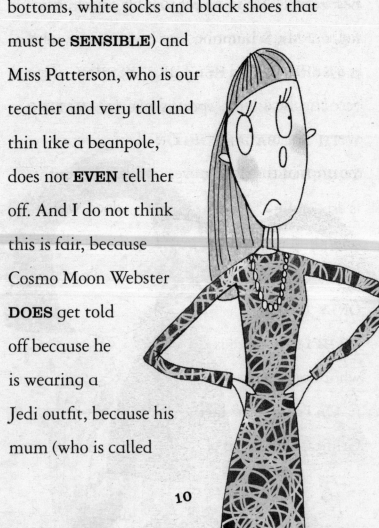

Sunflower, even though her real name is Barbara) believes in **FREEDOM** and **SELF-EXPRESSION**. And I get told off for wearing wellies, which is not because my mum believes in **FREEDOM** and **SELF-EXPRESSION**, it is because one of my shoes is down the drain after I was testing to see if it fitted through the gaps in the drain cover and it turns out it does, which I tell Miss Patterson.

And I also tell her that the wellies are very **SENSIBLE**, especially if it rains, but she does not agree. And Bridget Grimes, who mostly says annoying things like "*I would not do that if I were you, Penelope Jones*", says something else which is very annoying, which is:

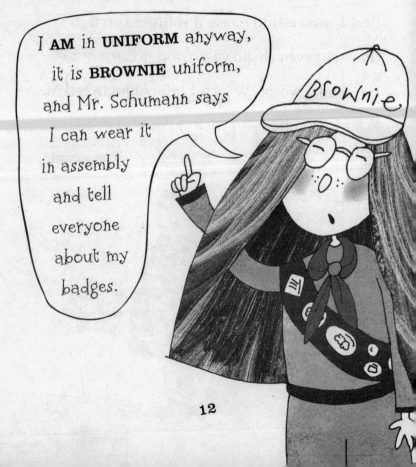

I **AM** in **UNIFORM** anyway, it is **BROWNIE** uniform, and Mr. Schumann says I can wear it in assembly and tell everyone about my badges.

And this is completely true, because in assembly Mr. Schumann makes Bridget Grimes stand up and show everyone her badges, and she has one for agility and one for science investigating and one for being a friend to the animals, even though I have seen her tread on a worm. Which I am trying to tell Mr. Schumann about by sticking my hand up and saying "Me, me", and also Cosmo is wanting to say something and is sticking his hand up and saying "Me, me", but it is not about Bridget, it is about Henry Potts (who is Cosmo's mortal enemy and who is poking him with a ruler).

But Mr. Schumann cannot seem to see me and Cosmo even though we are not wearing capes of invisibility and Cosmo is actually wearing the Jedi outfit (which is very **VISIBLE**), because he is still talking and what he is saying is that being a **BROWNIE** is all about **DOING YOUR BEST** and **TRYING TO HELP**

without expecting a thank you back. And then he also says,

Penelope Jones and Cosmo Moon Webster, I am **SICK AND TIRED** of you creating a **KERFUFFLE** in assembly. That is the fifth time this week, so you will have to spend playtime doing some thinking **INSIDE** instead of playing **OUTSIDE**.

So at playtime we do our **THINKING**, which is:

1. We would rather be outside because we can see Luke Bruce on the climbing frame and he is upside down and dangling by one leg which is **AMAZING** and we think we would like to try it.

b) Are elves real?

iii) Who would win in a fight between Optimus Prime, leader of the Autobots, and a Tyrannosaurus rex?

Which is when Mr. Schumann comes into the classroom and asks us what we are **THINKING**. And I say we are **THINKING** about whether Optimus Prime, leader of the Autobots, would beat a Tyrannosaurus rex in a fight if the Tyrannosaurus had rocket-powered boots on. Which Mr. Schumann says is not the sort of **THINKING** he was **THINKING** about and in fact we should be **THINKING** about what we can learn from Bridget Grimes, i.e. **DOING OUR BEST** and **TRYING TO BE HELPFUL**. Which I am not too happy about because normally I do not like learning things from Bridget Grimes, because normally it is things like *"If you carry on doing that it will get stuck"* (which it did). Only I

THINK I am actually quite keen on **DOING MY BEST** and **TRYING TO HELP**, and so does Cosmo, and so we decide we are going to be **BROWNIES**.

Only Bridget Grimes says Cosmo cannot be a Brownie because he is not a **GIRL** and that I cannot be a Brownie because I am not usually **DOING MY BEST**, I am usually doing things like throwing rubbers at Henry Potts. So Cosmo says he will get his mum to have a one-woman sit-in protest to let boys into Brownies (because she is very keen on one-woman sit-in protests). And I say I am going to stop throwing rubbers at Henry Potts, and I am going to **DO MY BEST** and **TRY TO HELP** instead, and we will both be Brownies before Bridget knows it.

And so for all the rest of the day I do not throw a rubber at Henry Potts and nor does Cosmo, even though Henry throws all sorts of mortal-enemy things at **US**, e.g.:

1. A protractor

b) A pencil with a troll on the end

3. A pot of superglue, which hits Alexander Pringle, who wears age 14 clothes even though he is nine and who is eating a lemon tart, and a bit of tart gets stuck and he goes quite reddish and so Cosmo **TRIES TO HELP**, i.e. he hits him on the back, and the tart flies out again.

And we are utterly **PLEASED AS PUNCH**.

But some people are not pleased, e.g. Alexander

Pringle who is still hungry. And Henry Potts, who gets sent to Mr. Schumann and has to write a hundred lines saying *I will not throw things at other children*. And Bridget Grimes, who starts to cry because her hair (which is very long and actually reaches her waist and she is always swishing it and saying "My hair actually reaches my waist, Penelope Jones") has got lemon tart and also glue stuck in it and Miss Patterson has to cut a bit of it out with craft scissors.

★ ★ ★ ★

The next day someone else is also utterly not

PLEASED AS PUNCH and it is my mum, because:

1. Dr. Cement has got a crisis with his filing

cabinet because he has lost Mrs.

Nougat and her bunions

somewhere in the Bs

by mistake and Mum

has to go to the office

on her day off.

2. Daisy (who is my big sister and

who is utterly

annoying) is

being doubly

annoying because she

wants to wear her swan

outfit to Lucy B. Finnegan's fancy dress party tonight, only there is chocolate porridge on it from my experiment at breakfast.

c) Dad is playing golf and the last time he did that he hit Mr. Butterworth on the head with a ball, who forgot who he was for three hours and especially forgot that he was married to Mrs. Butterworth in the post office, although Dad says that was a good thing and I agree because Mrs. Butterworth has a moustache and a beady eye (which is mostly on me).

So Cosmo says,

Do not fear, Janet, we will come to your rescue and **DO OUR BEST** and **TRY TO HELP**.

Only Mum says she has enough to worry about without me and Cosmo trying to do anything, and also if Cosmo calls her Janet one more time she may well have a conniption fit. (Only we do not know what this is, so we look it up and it is a tantrum for grown-ups and Cosmo decides he is quite **KEEN** on conniption fits and will definitely call her Janet again when she gets back from Dr. Cement's.)

And that is when I have my first **BRILLIANT IDEA™**, which is that we will **DO OUR BEST** and **TRY TO HELP** but we will do it secretly without expecting a thank you back, which is even more Brownie-like so they will definitely have to let us in for sure even though Cosmo is a boy.

So what we do is we make a list of all the

HELPFUL things we could do around the house, i.e.:

1. Do the washing-up because everything is quite hard and brown and lumpy with chocolate porridge.

b) Do the washing, because that is also quite hard and brown and lumpy, especially Daisy's swan outfit.

c) Feed Barry, who is Gran's cat, and who is right now eating a hard brown lump of chocolate porridge even though Mum says he must have **CAT BISCUITS AND CAT BISCUITS ONLY**.

Only then I remember that I am not allowed to touch the dishwasher for a lot of reasons, so we cannot do number **1**. And Gran says there are no cat biscuits because I used them up yesterday when I was trying to make a model of Krakatoa (which is a very tall volcano, and the exact colour of cat biscuits, only I do not think it melts when you pour lava on it, especially if the lava is actually custard), so we cannot do number **c)**.

But Cosmo says Barry is actually doing the washing-up with his tongue so if we let him eat all the porridge in fact we are being **HELPFUL**, which is very true. So we decide we will just do **b)**, which is *Do the washing*, and I am not banned from the washing machine yet which Mum says is a **MIRACLE** and Dad says is only a matter of time.

So we get all the washing in the washing basket and put it in the machine and get the box of washing powder and put quite a lot of that in too (because the porridge is very lumpy and also there are Dad's red socks in there, only they are a bit black from the time I used them to put shoe polish on my face when we were pretending to be aliens from Venus). And then we have an argument because Cosmo says he will be in charge of the machine knobs because he is a boy and a week older, and I say I will be in charge because the machine is in my kitchen. And then he says,

No I am.

And I say,

No I am.

And then we decide whoever can get a piece of chocolate porridge to stick to the ceiling will be in charge, and it is me because Cosmo's falls onto Gran's head who is asleep and amazingly it does not wake her up even though it is very hard. And so I put the machine on **HOT** and am feeling extremely **HELPFUL**.

Only then something **NOT AT ALL HELPFUL** happens, which is that bubbles are coming out of the machine like **MAD**, which is very unusual because it absolutely **NEVER** happens when Mum does the washing, which is a shame because it is actually very pretty.

Only soon it is also actually very messy and there are bubbles in places bubbles should not be, e.g. halfway up the chair legs. Which is when I have my second **BRILLIANT IDEA™**, which is to **SUCK** up the bubbles with a vacuum cleaner, only Cosmo says vacuum cleaners are not meant for wet things and he knows because Mr. Schumann has told him so and also banned him from ever using the school vacuum cleaner again. But I say our vacuum cleaner is a special one that can suck up water and shampoo carpets because Mum said it would be useful with all the spillages which are not actually my **FAULT**, they are just **ACCIDENTS**.

So we get the special vacuum cleaner and Cosmo says this time he is in charge because he is very keen on vacuuming and also because he has just got some porridge to stick to the kitchen window.

And I do not argue, only it turns out Cosmo may be **KEEN** on vacuuming but he is not **HELPFUL** at vacuuming, because as well as the bubbles he sucks up some things that are not meant to be sucked, e.g.:

1. Four drawing pins

2. A plastic monkey

c) Some chocolate porridge

And then another **NOT HELPFUL** thing happens, which is that the vacuum cleaner does not seem very happy with the drawing pins and the monkey and the chocolate porridge and the bubbles inside because it does an explosion and smoke comes out of it, which Cosmo says is excellent and like Krakatoa. But I do not **THINK** Mum will **THINK** so.

And so we decide to stop vacuuming and
to hang out the washing, only another **NOT
HELPFUL** thing has happened, which is that
quite a lot of the washing is not the colour it
was when it went in, i.e. it has
SOMEHOW gone **PINK**.

And then we are utterly **FLUMMOXED** because Dad does not like wearing pink shirts and also because Daisy says pink is her worst colour and that she would **RATHER PERISH** than ever wear it and so would Lucy B. Finnegan. Cosmo says if Daisy did perish I would get her bedroom and her microphone and her collection of plastic zoo animals, and I **THINK** this is true, but I also **THINK** this is not very **HELPFUL** and that we will definitely not be allowed into Brownies. So then Cosmo has his

BRILLIANT IDEA™

which is to dye the clothes blue, because blue is Daisy's third-best colour after yellow, and sparkle, and he knows how to dye things because

Sunflower has dyed all their sheets purple because of the **FREEDOM** and **SELF-EXPRESSION**. Only I say that Mum is not quite so keen on **FREEDOM** and **SELF-EXPRESSION** so we do not have any dye, and so we are racking our heads to think of where to get some when Cosmo has another **BRILLIANT IDEA™**, which is that ink is quite a lot like dye and so we can use that instead. And we do definitely have a lot of ink because of the time I knocked over a bottle of blackcurrant squash in the post office and Mrs. Butterworth saw it with her beady eye and said Dad would have to pay for the damaged goods, which was eleven Get Well Soon cards, two Famous Castles notebooks, and seven bottles of ink.

And so we get the blue ink and the pink washing and we take it all upstairs to the bath and we fill it with water and put everything in. And it is **COMPLETELY** amazing because almost immediately everything changes colour, including Dad's shirts and the swan outfit and the best tablecloth, only they are not blue, they are a sort of purplish colour, but I say that is okay because purplish is Daisy's fifth-best colour and she will not **PERISH**. And we are swirling the ink round the bath like **MAD**, which is when we notice that our hands have changed colour too. And then I have my next

BRILLIANT IDEA™,

which is to get in the bath because then we will

definitely look like aliens from Venus and Mum
will not be cross about shoe polish on socks.

And so we do. We get completely in the bath
in our pants and vests and are saying mostly
things like,

Greetings from Venus,
take me to your leader...

(which is what aliens sound like) when there is
another sound from downstairs, which I think
could be an alien or it could be Mum because
the sound is a scream sort of sound. And then
I know it is not aliens because the next sound is,

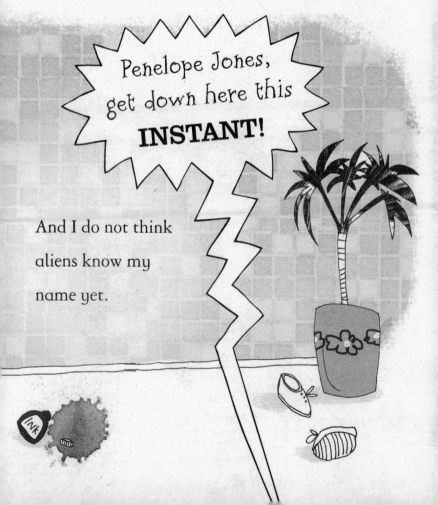

Penelope Jones,
get down here this
INSTANT!

And I do not think
aliens know my
name yet.

So we do go downstairs and the voice is definitely my mum who says she has already **HAD IT UP TO HERE** because of several things, i.e.:

1. That she has spent all morning looking for Mrs. Nougat's bunions **ONLY** to find they are filed under F for **FEET**.

2. That Dad has hit **HIMSELF** on the head with a golf ball and has forgotten how to drive and what his name is, so she has had to pick him up from the golf club.

c) That Daisy and Lucy B. Finnegan have decided they are **NOT** going to be swans **AFTER ALL**, they are going to be pop stars, which is another costume **ENTIRELY**.

So she is **DEFINITELY** not in the mood to come home and find that there are **BUBBLES** where **BUBBLES** should not be, that the vacuum cleaner will not vacuum any more, and that me and Cosmo Moon Webster have turned **BLUE**.

And Dad is not in the mood for anything because he is not even sure he lives here any more.

And Daisy is not in the mood to find her swan outfit all blue and the plastic monkey all melted and black and says,

It is all your fault, Penelope Jones, you are such a complete **MORON**.

And I say it is not my fault, I was only **DOING MY BEST** and trying to be **HELPFUL** so that I can join Brownies and wear my uniform to assembly like Bridget Grimes and get a badge for agility and one for being a friend to the animals. Only then Mum says that I **CANNOT** join Brownies even if I am a friend to the animals, because it is in the village hall and I am not allowed in the village hall for another two months because of the time I accidentally let Mrs. Jubilee's chickens into the kitchen, but it was only because they looked cold. So then I am not in the mood for anything at all, especially not being **HELPFUL** or **DOING MY BEST**. Which Mum says is frankly a relief.

But **SOMEONE** is in the mood, and that is Cosmo Moon Webster. Because he says Mum has definitely had a conniption fit and he didn't even have to call her **JANET**.

Sometimes I do not like being Penelope Jones,

and absolutely wish I was Cosmo Moon Webster, who is my best friend (even though he is a week older than me and a boy). This is because of several things:

1. He does not have to wear a skirt, not **EVER**, unless he chooses. Which he did once, to school, because his mum Sunflower (who is actually called Barbara) believes in **FREEDOM** and **SELF-EXPRESSION** and wrote a note to Mr. Schumann our headmaster to tell him so.

2) He can touch his nose with the tip of his tongue and I have practised for two hours and I still cannot do it, not even **CLOSE**.

iii. He is an **ONLY** child, i.e. he does not have a big sister.

Cosmo says actually in fact he would like a big sister because it would be nice to have someone to play war or have a beetle race with, because right now he is very **KEEN** on beetle races.

But I do not think he would like to have my big sister, i.e. Daisy Jones, because:

a. She is **NOT** keen on beetles, or ants, or worms and is absolutely never playing war because she is too busy being a pop star with Lucy B. Finnegan, who is her best friend (and who I have seen get her finger stuck down a plughole).

b) She is mostly saying, "Penelope Jones,

it is all your fault, you are such a complete **MORON**", i.e. she is **VERY** irritating.

But this week she is **DOUBLY** irritating and it is all because of the **HORMONES**.

HORMONES are chemicals that are inside you when you are a teenager and make you do things like grow hair in your armpits, and say "I hate you, you are ruining my life". And no one is allowed to say anything about it except "It is just her **HORMONES**". Which is not fair, because when I said I hated Bridget Grimes (who is top of the class and Mr. Schumann's favourite) because she had beaten me at Boggle three times in a row, no one said "It is just her **HORMONES**", they said "Penelope Jones, that is a very unkind thing to say".

Mum says the sooner the **TEENAGE YEARS** are all over the better. But Daisy's do not even start for one year, three months and eleven days, so it is a long wait. Anyway, what the **HORMONES** have done now is that they have made Daisy be **IN LOVE**. **IN LOVE** means she is completely wanting to kiss a boy, and that boy is called Joshua Bottomley and he sits next to her in French and smells of air freshener and once beat George Helmet at running even though George has the longest legs in Year 7 and maybe the world. I say he does not sound very **LOVELY** because I do not like air fresheners or French and I bet he can't touch his nose with the tip of his tongue.

But Gran says love is **BLIND**, e.g. Grandpa Jones (who is dead now, but wasn't before) looked a bit like an orang-utan, and couldn't swim, but she still **LOVED** him.

And Mum says Dad wears creased trousers
and drinks orange juice from the carton, even
though she has told him a million times that it
is unhygienic, but she still **LOVES** him.

And Dad is possibly about to say something
about Mum but she makes her lips go thin and so
he changes his mind and says Dr. Cement has eyes
like hard-boiled eggs which is why everyone calls
him Dr. Bugeye, but Mrs. Cement still **LOVES** him.

And I say I hope I am **NEVER** in love, because it is **BLIND** and what if I am in **LOVE** with e.g. Henry Potts, who is Cosmo's mortal enemy and is always throwing rubbers at him; or Brady O'Grady, who has patterns shaved in his hair and a dog called Killer; or Fraser Forks, who does not even go to school and only eats vegetables. And Mum says she hopes not either, because I am enough bother as it is. Only **FOR ONCE** I am not as much bother as Daisy.

Because what happens is that Daisy is wanting Joshua Bottomley to come to tea. But because of the **HORMONES** she is also **NOT** wanting a lot of other things, i.e.:

a. Dad is **NOT** allowed to say that he could have been a deep-sea diver, or a stuntman, or a pickle farmer if he hadn't met Mum, because it will be **EMBARRASSING** and she would **RATHER PERISH**.

2. Mum is **NOT** allowed to talk about Mrs. Nougat's bunions, because it will be **EMBARRASSING** and she would **RATHER PERISH**.

3) Gran is **NOT** allowed to let Barry, who is her cat, eat the tea, because it is **CAT BISCUITS** and **CAT BISCUITS ONLY**, and also it will be **EMBARRASSING** and she would **RATHER PERISH**.

iv. I am **NOT EVEN** allowed in the house, because it will be **EMBARRASSING** and she would **RATHER PERISH**.

NO PENNY

And **AMAZINGLY** Mum says yes to **ALL** of these things, because Gran will be at Arthur Peason's house playing rummy, Dad will be busy solving a crisis to do with some yellow lines on the road, and I will be at Cosmo's eating nettle jelly. Which I say is not fair because I am not even **KEEN** on nettle jelly and also because when I asked if the man who sleeps in the bus shelter could come to tea, Mum said no he could not. But Mum says it is not the same and anyway, it is Daisy's **HORMONES**.

And I am not in any way happy about Daisy's **HORMONES**, and decide I would very much like to have some **HORMONES** for myself, and so that is when I have my **BRILLIANT IDEA™**, which is to invent some. And so I go to Cosmo's house, because he has a chemistry set **AND** is actually allowed to use it, because of the **FREEDOM** and **SELF-EXPRESSION**. I have a chemistry set but I am **NOT** allowed to use it, although it is not to do with **FREEDOM** and **SELF-EXPRESSION**, it is to do with the time I tried to invent monkeys, and the time I tried to invent gold, and the time I wasn't trying to invent anything but I accidentally invented something that made the house fill with purple smoke and we had to call the fire brigade.

And Cosmo is also very **KEEN** on inventing some hormones (although in fact he is **KEEN** on inventing anything, especially if it is the first-ever time machine made out of a bus, some tinfoil and an alarm clock – only Mr. Schumann has told him a million times that that will **NEVER** happen) and so we get out the chemistry set and also a lot of things from the kitchen cupboards, e.g.:

a) Some home-made ginger jam

ii) Some green food colouring that did not hurt animals when it was being made

c. Some home-made lemonade

4. Some organic chickpea flour

V. Some wheat-free and sugar-free biscuits

The jam and biscuits are not to experiment with, they are to eat, because according to Mr. Schumann your brain needs a teaspoon of sugar an hour to work properly, only this does not mean Alexander Pringle is allowed to eat jam sandwiches in the classroom, it means eating **SENSIBLY**. But Sunflower does not have a lot of sensible food and so it is jam on biscuits.

So we are using the kitchen table because that is **SENSIBLE**, and wearing our goggles for **SAFETY**, and Cosmo is wearing his white coat which is what inventors wear and I am wearing a silver cape which is what Captain Danger wears, because it is that or a Jedi outfit.

And we are inventing like **MAD**, i.e. we invent:

1. Green stuff
b) Fizzy stuff
3. Green fizzy stuff

But no hormones yet, so we decide to have our snack because it has been quite **ARDUOUS** and our brains might need more sugar, and so we eat eight biscuits and eight spoonfuls of jam. And that is when I have my **BRILLIANT IDEA™** Number 2, which is to use the jam for inventing after all, because it is quite sticky and also gloopy and I think hormones are definitely sticky or maybe gloopy.

And so what we do is we get the glass pot from
the chemistry set and in it we put:

1. The jam
2. The flour
c) The lemonade
iv. A biscuit that has broken
5. The green food colouring

And it is definitely gloopy, and a bit crunchy

as well, so we taste it but it does not taste like

HORMONES, it tastes

of lemon and ginger

and it definitely

does not make me

want to **PERISH**.

And Cosmo says this is because we have not
got the **SECRET INGREDIENT** and I say,
"What *is the* **SECRET INGREDIENT**?"
and he says he is not sure, and so we look in
the cupboards and Cosmo says it is definitely
NOT brown spaghetti or lentils or tomato juice.
And then we look in the fridge and Cosmo says
it is definitely **NOT** cheese with holes in or
nettle jelly. So then we look in the bathroom
but Sunflower says even though she believes in
FREEDOM and **SELF-EXPRESSION** she does
not believe in eating soap. So then I have my

Number 3, which is to ask Mrs. Butterworth at
the post office, because even though she is

always saying stuff like "I have got my beady eye on you" and has a moustache, she has also won the St Regina's church fete scone competition for two years in a row and it is down to her **SECRET INGREDIENT**.

Only when we get to the post office, Mrs. Butterworth is not completely **KEEN** on telling me her **SECRET INGREDIENT** because she says I will tell Gran and then Gran will win the scone competition and will walk around with her nose in the air.

And I say Gran does not cook scones, she does not even cook a boiled egg, she is mostly busy watching *Animal SOS* (which is a TV series where animals are always nearly dying but then they don't and it is **MIRACULOUS**). Plus she does not have her nose in the air because her back has gyp and so it is more towards the ground. And Mrs. Butterworth says in that case she **WILL** tell us the **SECRET INGREDIENT**, and it is bicarbonate of soda. And so we buy some, and Mrs. Butterworth says she will keep her beady eye on us anyway, but we do not mind because we are about to invent **HORMONES**.

And what we do when we get back to Cosmo's is we add **ALL** of the bicarbonate of soda to the glass pot. And this time something **DOES** happen. And it is that the green jammy stuff begins to foam. And it is not just a small amount of foam, it is quite largish and quite fast. And it is foaming all over the table, and onto the floor, and across the floor, and out of the door.

And Cosmo says it is definitely **ALIEN ECTOPLASM**, because he is quite **KEEN** on alien ectoplasm, but I taste it and it is very strange and not at all nice any more and I say it is definitely **HORMONES**. And it is true, because then I say,

I hate you.

And then Cosmo tastes some and he says,

No I hate **YOU**.

And we are **HATING** like **MAD** and that is when Sunflower comes in and decides she does not believe in **FREEDOM** and **SELF-EXPRESSION** so much today and that we will both have to have tea at my house after all. And I say it is **VICTORY NUMBER ONE** for the hormones and Cosmo agrees and so we put some of the **HORMONES** in the jam jar and go back to my house.

Only Daisy does not think this is a **VICTORY** at all because Joshua Bottomley is going to be here absolutely soon and me and Cosmo are quite covered in green jam and she will be **EMBARRASSED** and would **RATHER PERISH**. And I say it is not green jam, it is **HORMONES**, and also **I** would **RATHER PERISH**.

And Cosmo says **HE** would **RATHER PERISH**.
Only Mum says she is **UP TO HERE** with all
the **PERISHING** and to get upstairs and get
cleaned up before she **PERISHES** herself and
then **NO ONE** will have tea at all, **HORMONES**
or not.

And so we do, because even though we have eaten the biscuits and the jam we are quite tired with all the inventing and our brains definitely need more sugar, and possibly some fish fingers too.

Only when we get back downstairs we are very surprised because a lot of people have appeared from nowhere and Cosmo says maybe someone has invented the first-ever time machine made out of a bus and some tinfoil and an alarm clock, but Mum says no they have not, because that is **NEVER** going to happen. What **HAS** happened is that Gran has had an argument with Arthur Peason about the Jack of Spades and so **SHE** is here. And Dad has amazingly solved the crisis with the yellow lines but then has accidentally set off the fire alarm, so **HE** is here. And I say I hate them all and they have ruined my life. But Daisy says I do not, because **SHE** hates everyone and they have ruined **HER** life because now Joshua Bottomley will not be **IN LOVE** with her.

And for once I am thinking that Daisy is right, because when we are eating tea Joshua Bottomley is not looking at all **IN LOVE**, he is looking at Barry, who is eating a bowl of cereal. And also at me and Cosmo, because we are still wearing the white coat and the silver cape with the green jammy stuff on the front. And that is when I have my **BRILLIANT IDEA™** Number 4, which is to give Joshua Bottomley some extra **HORMONES** because then he will absolutely definitely be **IN LOVE**.

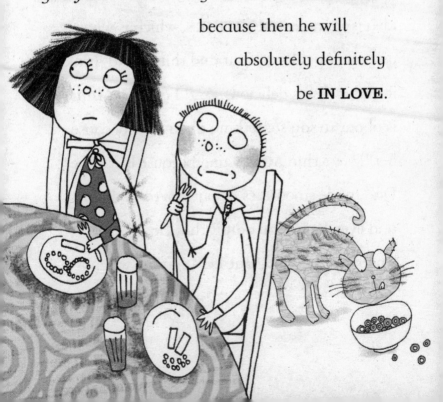

And so I am **RACKING MY BRAINS** about
how to give Joshua Bottomley the extra
hormones, because I do not think he will eat
green jam out of a jar, when Dad has one of his
BRIGHT IDEAS™,
which is a bit like a **BRILLIANT IDEA™**,
only Mum does not usually agree. And his
idea is to make **SMOOTHIES**, which is when
you mix up a lot of fruit and things and drink
it and it tastes delicious. And I can tell Mum
is about to say something about this because
her lips go thin **AGAIN** and because last time
Dad made smoothies he put Bovril in them
and even he had to admit that Bovril
smoothies are bad. But Dad says he will not

put any Bovril in them, he will just put bananas and milk and strawberries and his **SECRET INGREDIENT** in. Only his **SECRET INGREDIENT** is not the same as Mrs. Butterworth's **SECRET INGREDIENT**, it is **GREEN FOOD COLOURING**, because it turns the smoothie into alien ectoplasm. Which is when I have my next

BRILLIANT IDEA™,

which is to add the

HORMONES to Joshua

Bottomley's smoothie, because

it will be green and he will not

be able to tell the difference,

and then he will be

IN LOVE for sure.

And so I am helping Dad like **MAD** by stirring smoothies and Mum says it is nice to see me being so **USEFUL**, even if I am in a jammy cape. And everyone is happy, even Daisy, because she says her smoothie actually

tastes of fruit this time and
that Joshua Bottomley should
definitely try his. And he
does, only Joshua Bottomley

does not think it tastes of fruit,
because he goes
quite palish and is
sick on the table. And Gran says
maybe he is allergic to strawberries,
because Mrs. Gibbon is allergic
to strawberries and if
she eats even one her
tongue swells up and
she gets hives on her
thighs and nearly dies. And then
Joshua goes even more palish.

83

But Daisy says he is not allergic to strawberries because she has seen him eat a strawberry bootlace and he is not dead. And I say maybe it is not strawberries, it is **HORMONES**.

And Mum says,

WHAT hormones, Penelope Jones?

And I say the ones we invented at Cosmo's house and put in the smoothie to make him fall **IN LOVE**. And that is when Dad does his honking goose laugh. But Mum does not see the funny side, because she says it is very dangerous inventing things and making people drink them without telling them and we must **NEVER** do it again. And nor does Joshua Bottomley, who says can he go home please?

And nor does Daisy, who is definitely
EMBARRASSED and wanting to **PERISH**.
She says,

It is all your fault, Penelope Jones, you are such a **COMPLETE MORON**.

But for once I do not mind, because the next day she decides she is not **IN LOVE** with Joshua Bottomley, she is in love with George Helmet after all. It is her **HORMONES**.

Penny Dreadful

and the

New Girl

Mr. Schumann is our headmaster

and he is mostly saying things like, "Penelope Jones, I am **SICK AND TIRED** of telling you that chairs are for **SITTING** on, not **DANGLING UPSIDE DOWN** on, and if you do not **STOP** the dangling this **INSTANT** *I will be* **FORCED** to take away a gold star." Even though in actual fact he has already taken away **ALL** my gold stars this week for several things that were completely not my fault, e.g.:

1. Accidentally getting locked in the toilet because me and Cosmo were testing how super superglue was on the door and it turns out it is very super, which was a scientific experiment and so if you think about it I should **GET** a gold star, not have one taken away.

b) Accidentally getting Luke Bruce's duffel coat stuck on top of the apple tree because we

were having a competition to
see who had the superpower
of throwing, and it is me.

C. Accidentally
getting stuck up the
apple tree trying to fetch
Luke Bruce's duffel coat
back down again, which
meant Mr. Schumann had to
call the fire brigade (and they
were already cross about the
time they had to come to school
to rescue Gran's cat Barry,
who I brought in for show-and-tell
and who ran up the curtain in the
dinner hall and got stuck).

But I do not tell him this because this week Mr. Schumann is even more **SICK AND TIRED** than usual, because there is a **NEW GIRL** coming to our school and she is called Elsie Maud. Mr. Schumann says Elsie Maud's dad is someone especially **IMPORTANT**, so we must absolutely **SET AN EXAMPLE** and show her we are **KIND** and **CLEVER** and **CALM**, otherwise she will go to The Drabble Academy for Girls like my cousin Georgia May Morton-Jones, which has a swimming pool and Mandarin (which is not a fruit, it is a language).

I say she would be **MAD** to go to The Drabble Academy for Girls because they have to wear ties and hats, but Mr. Schumann is looking like he thinks it would be good if we wore ties and hats, only possibly not the policeman's helmet that Cosmo Moon Webster is wearing right now.

Anyway, Mr. Schumann asks us if we can be **TRUSTED** to **SET THE EXAMPLE** and be **KIND** and **CLEVER** and **CALM** and we all say

Yes.

Except for Alexander Pringle who cannot say anything because he is eating a jam sandwich, which Miss Patterson says is definitely **NOT** an example of anything.

And after that everyone is **RACKING THEIR HEADS** like **MAD** to guess who Elsie Maud's **IMPORTANT** dad is, e.g.:

1. Bridget Grimes, who is top of the class and Mr. Schumann's favourite, says he is probably the Prime Minister.

b) Brady O'Grady

(who has had an arrow shaved into his hair by Shaniqua Reynolds at Hair Today, only he moved and it looks more like a caterpillar) says he is probably Wayne Plane, number one footballer, because he is very **KEEN** on football.

3. Henry Potts, who is Cosmo Moon Webster's mortal enemy, says he is probably Maximus Terror, leader of the Zombiebots, because he is very **KEEN** on Maximus Terror.

Only Cosmo is not so keen on Maximus Terror so he throws a rubber at Henry Potts and it misses and hits Cherry Scarpelli on the nose, and she starts crying because she cannot be in the Broadley Junior May Queen Pageant with a bulgy nose.

And then Miss Patterson says we are definitely **NOT SETTING AN EXAMPLE** or being **KIND** or **CALM**. But I say we are being **CLEVER** because if he **IS** Maximus Terror then we will know we can defeat him with our laser-eyed Dogbots. But Miss Patterson does not agree and says it would be **CLEVERER** to get out our maths books and work out how long it will take to fill a bucket with water if the water is pouring in at half a litre every forty seconds.

How lo
will it
to fill
Water
Pouring

Anyway, when I get home I tell Mum and Dad and Daisy all about Elsie Maud and us **SETTING AN EXAMPLE** or she will go to The Drabble Academy for Girls even though they have hats and learn Mandarin. And Daisy says she is possibly the daughter of Clint Van Spangle, who is her favourite pop star **EVER** and that I have to get his autograph because then Lucy B. Finnegan will be **MAD** with jealousy.

Clint Van Spangle

And Dad says she is possibly the daughter of a famous Arctic explorer and that he could have been an Arctic explorer if he had not met Mum. Only Mum says he could not, because he does not like even a **BIT** of snow. And Aunt Deedee, who has come round to find a sock that belongs to Georgia May Morton-Jones, says if the famous father has any sense he will be sending Elsie Maud to The Drabble Academy for Girls by the end of the week anyway, because they have Mandarin, and a swimming pool, and hats, and also they have heard of the word **DISCIPLINE**. And I can tell Mum is about to say in fact Mr. Schumann has also heard of the word **DISCIPLINE** because her lips go a bit thinnish, but luckily then Gran puts on *Animal SOS*, and so Aunt Deedee goes home

because Georgia May is
only allowed to watch the
Maths Channel.

Anyway, we are **ALL**
watching *Animal SOS* and
this week it is all about a pet cow
called Hilda who has fallen down
a cliff and is
nearly dead,
but then the
helicopter rescue
unit winch her
up to safety in a
giant blanket and the
vet revives her and so
she does not die and it is

MIRACULOUS, which I know because Griff Hunt, who is the presenter, says so.

And that is when I have my

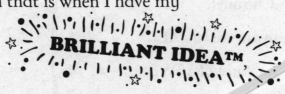

BRILLIANT IDEA™,

which is that in fact Elsie Maud's dad is Griff Hunt. Only Dad says no, he is sure Elsie Maud's dad is an Arctic explorer. And Daisy says if he is not Clint Van Spangle then she would **RATHER PERISH**. And Mum says she hopes he is anyone **BUT** Griff Hunt, because then the whole village will be full of TV people with their funny glasses and accents and clothes. But Gran is pleased as punch because she says if he **IS** Griff Hunt then she will never have to worry about Barry again,

not even when
he gets stuck
in the washing
machine or eats
wasps, because Griff
Hunt will be able to
revive him and shout "*It's a* **MIRACLE**".
And I think Gran is right and so I have
my second

BRILLIANT IDEA™,

which is to be best friends with Elsie Maud.
But I will not tell anyone except for Cosmo,
because otherwise they will all start bringing
in their pets that are nearly dying so that they
can be revived and **MIRACULOUS**.

✷ ✷ ✷ ✷

Only when I get to school the next day, a lot

of other people are wanting to be

best friends with Elsie Maud, e.g.:

1. Bridget Grimes,

who has brought her a book

about kings and queens.

b) Cherry Scarpelli,

who has brought her a tiara

with pink jewels in it, and a

roller skate.

c) Alexander

Pringle, who has brought

her a jam sandwich, a

biscuit shaped like a hippo,

and two sausage rolls.

But Miss Patterson says friendship is not about roller skates or books and it is definitely not about biscuits shaped like hippos, it is about being **KIND**. And also **CALM**, because Bridget Grimes and Cherry Scarpelli, who normally are completely **KEEN** on sitting next to each other, both want each other to move so Elsie Maud can sit next to them, and are both crying.

And Alexander Pringle is cross because Brady
O'Grady has eaten one of his sausage rolls
and so he is chasing Brady around the room
with a ruler. And Henry Potts is pretending to
be Maximus Terror and is using his
deathly shrinking ray on Cosmo
Moon Webster, only Cosmo says he is

wearing his cape of invisibility (which is actually a silver cape, and he is actually wearing it) and so he cannot be shrunk, and so they are arguing like **MAD**, and definitely **NOT SETTING AN EXAMPLE**.

Which is when Mr. Schumann walks in with

Elsie Maud, who
has hair that is
orange-coloured
and a lot of
freckles.

   And I can tell
immediately
that Mr.
Schumann is
**SICK AND
TIRED**, because
his face goes
quite palish,
and also
because he

tells everyone to **STOP** the **SHENANIGANS** and sit back down in their seats so that he can find Elsie Maud a chair.

And so everyone does sit down and they are sticking their hands up absolutely high and going,

Me, me, Mr. Schumann!

But for once I am completely quiet and still because I am very **MESMERIZED**. Which means I am staring, i.e. at Elsie Maud and her orange hair and freckles, which I think I would like very much, and also I would like the badge on her cardigan which is a kitten, which is a pet, which is **CLUE NUMBER 1**, and which means her dad is **DEFINITELY** Griff Hunt.

And then **MIRACULOUSLY** Miss Patterson says,

Penelope Jones is being **CALM** so maybe Elsie Maud can sit next to her.

Because there is an empty chair next to me because Cosmo has sat next to Henry Potts to annoy him by being invisible.

Only Mr. Schumann does not look so **KEEN** on this idea and he says maybe Bridget Grimes can swap with me and I can sit with Cherry Scarpelli. But Cherry Scarpelli is not so keen on **THIS** idea and starts crying even more. And also Elsie Maud is not keen on this idea because she sits right down next to me and Mr. Schumann does **NOT EVEN SAY ANYTHING**.

Anyway, what happens is that I am **PLEASED AS PUNCH** because what we are doing first is **ART** and we are doing **COLLABORATIVE COLLAGES**, which means

WORKING TOGETHER to stick a lot of stuff on a big bit of paper and absolutely **NO ARGUING**. And I say we should do a collage of a cow that is dead and being winched by a helicopter and Elsie Maud says this is a very **BRILLIANT** idea, which is **CLUE NUMBER 2**. And so I am cutting out a picture of a cow and sticking it upside down and Elsie Maud is squeezing red paint over it for blood.

Only then Henry Potts decides he needs red paint because him and Cosmo are doing a collage of Maximus Terror fighting some laser-eyed Dogbots, only they are not doing it very **COLLABORATIVELY** because Cosmo is mostly being invisible.

Only Elsie Maud says Maximus Terror does not have blood, he has green ectoplasm, and so Henry needs green paint.

And then there is a lot of arguing and saying

And

And Henry and Elsie Maud are both squeezing
paint all over the Maximus Terror picture and
also quite a bit over each other, and some gets

on Cherry Scarpelli's and Bridget Grimes's picture, which is of fairies on a rainbow. Only Cherry Scarpelli and Bridget Grimes are not **KEEN** on the blood **OR** ectoplasm on the fairies and they start crying, which is when Miss Patterson says we have done enough **COLLABORATION** for one day and maybe we should do **NATURE OBSERVATION** instead, which means looking at plants and minibeasts in the playground and collecting things in shoeboxes and **ABSOLUTELY NO FOOLING ABOUT ON THE CLIMBING FRAME**.

So we are outside, **ABSOLUTELY NOT** fooling around on the climbing frame and **ABSOLUTELY** looking at an earwig which is eating an ant, which we put in our nature shoebox. And I say,

And she says,

Maybe your dad could save the ant, Elsie Maud.

It would be **MIRACULOUS** because the ant is very dead.

Which is **CLUE NUMBER 3**. And I am about to do more clues when something very interesting happens, i.e. Cosmo **OBSERVES** some **NATURE** and it is a dead pigeon on the pavement behind the railings, which is when I have my next **BRILLIANT IDEA™**, which is to give Elsie Maud the dead pigeon and then her dad can **REVIVE** it, which will be **MIRACULOUS** and also **CLUE NUMBER 4**. And **AMAZINGLY** Elsie Maud agrees and so we are trying to reach the pigeon with a twig when Alexander Pringle says he will reach it for Elsie Maud with his **BARE HANDS**, because he has age-14 size arms and ours are only age-9 size. And Elsie Maud says this is a good idea, but what would be even better is if he also stuck his head through

the railings to see what he is doing. And
Alexander Pringle says he will do **ANYTHING**
for Elsie Maud, even cut off his arm. Which we
think might be a good idea for later because it
would be very interesting to see a cut-off arm,
but right now he can just stick his head through
the railings and get the dead pigeon. And

amazingly he **CAN** reach
the pigeon because of
the age-14 size arms,
but it turns out his
head is also age-14
size because it does
not want to come
out of the railings as
easily as it went in.

And then what happens is that Cosmo says he will save Alexander Pringle with his cape of invisibility and invisible arms. So he is pulling very hard on Alexander Pringle with his invisible arms, but all that is happening is that Alexander Pringle's face is getting very red and he is saying a lot, which is when Mr. Schumann comes outside to see what all the **SHENANIGANS** are.

And completely immediately he is **SICK AND TIRED** because he says now he will have to call the fire brigade **AGAIN**, and also because it is clear we have not been **SETTING AN EXAMPLE** for Elsie Maud or being **KIND** or **CALM** or **CLEVER**.

And so it will be singing practice for the rest of the day, because if our brains are **BUSY** looking at songbooks and our voices are **BUSY** singing, then we will not be able to be **BUSY** creating **SHENANIGANS**.

And so we do singing all afternoon and there are no **SHENANIGANS** except that we are singing a song about conkers and Elsie Maud says she can in fact do the tune by **BURPING**. And she does and it is brilliant and then everyone is burping like **MAD**, except for Bridget Grimes who is still gloomy about the ectoplasm on the fairies, and except for Alexander Pringle who is still stuck in the railings.

Only then Elsie Maud does a really
big burp and a bit of pink custard
comes back up, which is when
Mr. Schumann comes in with a
tall man with orange hair
and freckles and
who is almost
DEFINITELY
Elsie Maud's
dad and
definitely **NOT**
Griff Hunt.

And the Mr. **NOT**-Griff-Hunt is completely not happy about several things:

1. Because the floor is quite covered in green and red paint and also pink custard sick, and so is Elsie Maud.

b) Because there is a boy with his head stuck in the railings in the playground.

iii. Because Elsie Maud's **COLLABORATIVE** collage is of a dead cow being winched by a helicopter.

iv. Because Miss Patterson has given him Elsie Maud's nature shoebox and inside is an earwig, an ant and a dead pigeon.

And Mr. Schumann goes very pale and says,

Who is **RESPONSIBLE** for this?

And I am quite **KEEN** on being **RESPONSIBLE** so I say,

I am. Because we thought Elsie Maud's dad was maybe possibly Griff Hunt, who is on *Animal SOS*, which is this TV series where animals almost die and then they don't and it is **MIRACULOUS**. And he is going to revive the pigeon and the ant and shout 'It's a **MIRACLE**'.

Only Elsie Maud's dad says he is not going to revive the ant or the pigeon because he is not Griff Hunt. And he is not a lot of other people either:

a) The Prime Minister
b) Wayne Plane
3. Maximus Terror
iv) Clint Van Spangle
5. An Arctic explorer

But he absolutely **IS** important because he is the new vicar at St Regina's church.

When I get home I tell everyone about Mr. **NOT**-Griff-Hunt and Dad is absolutely

disappointed that he is not an Arctic explorer
and Daisy is absolutely disappointed that he
is not Clint Van Spangle and Mum is
absolutely disappointed that I put a dead
pigeon in a box and got Alexander Pringle's
head stuck in railings.

Only when I get to school the next day,
Alexander Pringle's head is not in the railings
any more and in fact the
railings are not there **EITHER**
and nor is Elsie Maud, because
she has gone to The Drabble
Academy for Girls after
all. Which means
Mr. Schumann is very
SICK AND TIRED indeed.

But he is not as **SICK AND TIRED** as Aunt Deedee. Because when I get home from school she is ringing and is very cross because Georgia May Morton-Jones has got her head stuck in some railings, and for once it is completely **NOT MY FAULT**. It is Elsie Maud's.

The End

Penny Dreadful's Top 5 Tips for Survival

Sometimes it is very **ARDUOUS** being a

MAGNET FOR DISASTER. Especially if

you are extra specially magnetic, i.e. like me.

But even though it is **ARDUOUS**, it is also

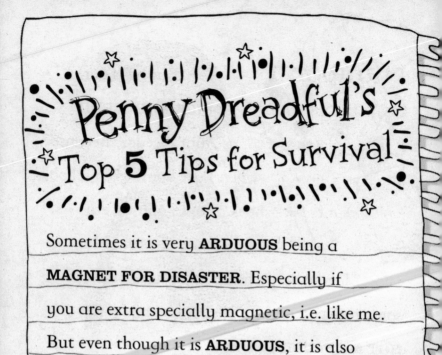

very **INFORMATIVE**,

i.e. I have learned

some important

TOP TIPS

about how to

avoid complete

CATASTROPHE.

Number 1

Get a DISGUISE

It is completely
important not to
look like me, i.e.
Penelope Jones,
when I am being
very magnetic,
e.g. accidentally

knocking over a teetering pile of envelopes
in the post office. So sometimes I dress up as
Cosmo, i.e. in a Jedi outfit and wellies, because
it completely confuses Mrs. Butterworth's
beady eye and however hard she **RACKS**
her brain she is **FLUMMOXED** as to who to
shout at.

Another good disguise is dressing up as a burglar, because burglars wear balaclavas which **COMPLETELY** cover up their face.

Although it is possible you would get shouted at for being a burglar anyway.

Number 2
Collect COLLATERAL, i.e. money

Coins are **EVERYWHERE**, e.g. on the ground outside the post office, down the back of the sofa and mostly in Dad's trouser pocket.

Collect them **ALL** because you never know

when you might need them for:

1. Paying people back, e.g. your Aunt Deedee

when you have accidentally broken a glass

vase or phoned Russia for instance.

b) Buying essential supplies

like biscuits or liquorice sticks.

iii. Playing ludo, because you have

used the actual plastic counters to

flick at your mortal enemy.

Number 3
Be PREPARED for EVERY EVENTUALITY

DISASTERS are **EVERYWHERE** and you never

know when you might be super-magnetic,

so it is completely important to have a box

of useful things for **EVERY EVENTUALITY**,

i.e. anything, e.g.:

a) **COLLATERAL** (see above).

2. **A DISGUISE** (see above).

3. Biscuits (for **ARDUOUS**

JOURNEYS).

4. A bottle of washing-up liquid and a

sponge (for when you have spilled something,

or accidentally drawn some Roman soldiers

marching along the kitchen wall).

e) A torch (for when you have accidentally

blown up the vacuum cleaner by trying to suck

up the washing-up liquid, and all the lights

have gone off).

Number 4

Find a TRUSTY SCAPEGOAT

This means someone else to **BLAME**, e.g. in our house everyone mostly blames me, even though it is not usually my fault, it is that I am a **MAGNET FOR DISASTER**. So I usually blame Barry the cat, because he is most often eating things that are **NOT** cat biscuits. E.g. when Daisy said, "Where is my last cherry chocolate, Penelope Jones? I **KNOW** it is you who has eaten it," I said, "But in fact perhaps it is not I, it is **BARRY**, because he is completely **KEEN** on cherries and chocolate, so ha!"

Number 5

Get a FAITHFUL FRIEND

If you are very magnetic like me, it is **COMPLETELY** important to have a faithful friend, which is not the same thing as a scapegoat, and is also not the same as a dog, (especially not one that isn't yours but which you have found outside the post office only it is not lost at all) but e.g. Cosmo Moon Webster. Because faithful friends will always stand up for you, even when you have accidentally exploded custard in their microwave, and even if they are a boy and exactly a week older than you.

My
Faithful Friend

Everybody Loves Penny!

"Penny is an exciting and entertaining character who always has **BRILLIANT IDEAS**... If Penny was my **BFF** then life would never be dull."

Rachel, aged 9

"Penny Dreadful stories are very funny and exciting. It is a brilliant series."

Polly, aged 10

"I liked Penny because she's naughty, but in a way she's also funny too! I did not like Mrs. Butterworth because she's got a moustache."

Millie, aged 8

"I think Penny Dreadful is, well, dreadfully funny. (She sounds a bit like my brother — hee hee.) PS I'm turning a little dreadful too."

Islay, aged 8

"I think Penny Dreadful is a brilliant book! I learned 'e.g'. means 'for example'. I learned 'i.e.' means 'that is'."

Bryn, aged 8

"A hilariously brilliant read!"

Anastasia, aged 11

"I loved Penny Dreadful, especially in **'PENNY DREADFUL BECOMES A HAIRDRESSER'**. And the lady with the moustache. Fantastico!"

Leila, aged 7

"I love Penny Dreadful, she is brilliant and very funny."

Iona, aged 6

"I wanted to read on and on and on...it was <u>soooo</u> good."

Matt, aged 8

"This book is funny and full of **BRILLIANT IDEAS** and I like the way it uses '**E.G.**' all the time!"

Megan Emily, aged 6

"Here are some of the things I enjoyed about the book:

1. I liked it when Penny and Cosmo tried to shave Barry the cat (the coolest cat ever).
b) Does Penny ever comb her hair?
3. Where did Cosmo get his Jedi suit... I want one!
iv. I liked Mrs. Butterworth at the post office and her moustache!"

Gruffudd, aged 10

Joanna Nadin

wrote this book –
and lots of others
like it. She is small,
funny, clever,
sneaky and musical.

Before she became a writer, she wanted to be a
champion ballroom dancer or a jockey, but she
was actually a lifeguard at a swimming pool,
a radio newsreader, a cleaner in an old people's
home, and a juggler. She likes Marmite on toast
for mains breakfast, and jam on toast for
pudding. Her perfect day would involve baking,
surfing, sitting in cafes in Paris, and playing
with her daughter – who reminds her
a lot of Penny Dreadful…

Jess Mikhail

illustrated this book.
She loves creating funny
characters with bright
colours and fancy

patterns to make people smile.
Her favourite place is her tiny home, where she
lives with her tiny dog and spends lots of time
drawing, scanning, scribbling, printing, stamping,
and sometimes using her scary computer. She
loves to rummage through a good car boot sale
or a charity shop to find weird and
wonderful things. A perfect day for
her would have to involve a sunny
beach and large amounts of curry
and ice cream (not together).

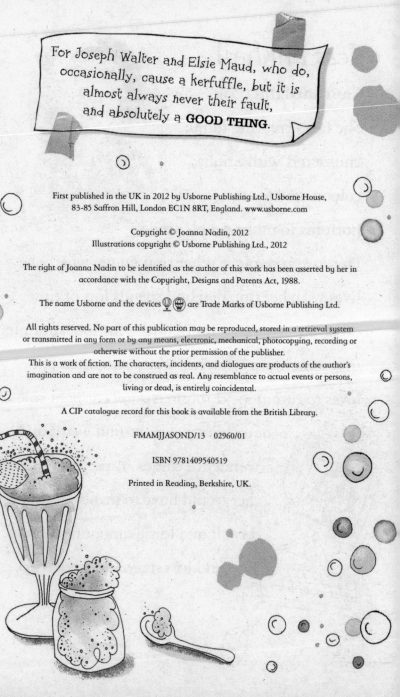

For Joseph Walter and Elsie Maud, who do, occasionally, cause a kerfuffle, but it is almost always never their fault, and absolutely a **GOOD THING**.

First published in the UK in 2012 by Usborne Publishing Ltd., Usborne House, 83-85 Saffron Hill, London EC1N 8RT, England. www.usborne.com

A CIP catalogue record for this book is available from the British Library.

FMAMJJASOND/13 · 02960/01

ISBN 9781409540519

Printed in Reading, Berkshire, UK.